The Boxcar Children Mysteries

THE MYSTERY OF THE RUNAWAY GHOST

created by
GERTRUDE CHANDLER WARNER

Illustrated by Hodges Soileau

Albert Whitman & Company
Chicago, Illinois

Contents

CHAPTER 1

Shadowbox

"Grandfather should be home soon," said six-year-old Benny. He pressed his nose against the living room window. "Any minute now, we'll find out about the surprise!" He sounded excited.

Ten-year-old Violet came up behind her younger brother. "I wonder what kind of surprise it is." She looked out the window, too. There was no sign of Grandfather yet.

Jessie, who was twelve, was placing napkins around the dining room table. "It's not like Grandfather to be so mysterious," she said. "Tell us again what he said on the phone, Henry."

"He didn't say much," said Henry, as he poured lemonade into tall glasses. "He wouldn't even give me a hint. He just said he was bringing home pizza for dinner — pizza *and* a surprise." At fourteen, Henry was the oldest of the Alden children.

"One thing's for sure," said Jessie. "Grandfather's surprises are *always* fun." At that, Watch, the family dog, looked up and barked in agreement.

Violet had a faraway look in her eye. "Remember when Grandfather surprised us with the boxcar?"

The others nodded and smiled. After their parents died, the four Alden children had run away. They discovered an abandoned boxcar in the woods and made it their home. Then their grandfather, James Alden, found them and brought them to live with him in his big white house in Greenfield. He had the boxcar moved to his backyard as a special surprise for his grandchildren. The Aldens often used the boxcar as a clubhouse.

"Well, surprises always make me hungry," Benny said. "I hope Grandfather gets a really big pizza."

"Oh, Benny!" Jessie laughed. "*Everything* makes you hungry."

Just then, James Alden walked in the door. He was holding a pizza box from Joe's Restaurant. "Ready to dig in?" he asked, smiling fondly at his grandchildren. "I ordered an extra-large topped with special tomato sauce, extra cheese, and pepperoni."

Benny let out a cheer. "That's my favorite kind!"

The children forgot all about the surprise for a while as they helped themselves to pizza. Finally, Grandfather sat back in his chair and said, "Are you ready to hear my news?"

Henry, Jessie, Violet, and Benny looked up expectantly. "Yes! What is it, Grandfather?" Violet asked.

"I was talking to my friend Fran Russell

today. I have some business to take care of in Cedarburg, Wisconsin, and I thought I'd stop by to see her while I'm there." Grandfather took a sip of his lemonade. "She invited the four of you to come with me and spend a few days with her at Shadowbox. What do you think?"

Everyone thought it was a great idea. The children had often heard their grandfather speak of his good friend Fran and her old stone house, Shadowbox.

"Shadowbox sure is a weird name for a house," Benny said.

"The name fits, Benny," said Grandfather, smiling over at his youngest grandson. "When you see the house, you'll know what I mean." He helped himself to another slice of pizza.

Henry was curious. "How old is Shadowbox, Grandfather?"

Grandfather took a bite of his pizza and chewed thoughtfully for a moment. Then he said, "As I recall, Fran's ancestors built Shadowbox back in the 1850s. It's been in the family ever since. Fran takes great pride in her home," he added. "And in the family ghost."

The children all looked at their grandfather in surprise. "The family *what*?" said Benny, his eyes round.

Grandfather's eyes crinkled with amusement. "According to the story, Shadowbox is haunted by a runaway ghost."

"What do you mean?" asked Henry.

"Is the ghost one of Fran's ancestors?" Jessie asked at the same time.

Then Violet chimed in, "What kind of ghost runs away?"

Grandfather couldn't help laughing as he held up a hand to slow them down. "You'll hear all about the runaway ghost when you get to Shadowbox."

Benny wiped tomato sauce from his chin. "Won't you tell us now?" he pleaded.

Grandfather shook his head. "Fran loves to tell visitors about the family ghost. I don't want to spoil it for her."

Benny was deep in thought. "Do you

think it's true?" he said at last. "Do you think Shadowbox is haunted?" He sounded uneasy.

"I doubt it, Benny," Grandfather said. "But Fran enjoys entertaining people, and a good ghost story is bound to get everyone's attention."

"It sure got *our* attention!" said Henry.

Benny nodded as he took the last bite of his pizza. "I can't wait to hear more about it."

"Well, you won't have to wait long," Grandfather told him. "Our flight leaves the day after tomorrow."

"Cedarburg isn't much farther," Jessie said, studying the map unfolded on her lap. She was sitting in the front seat of the car Grandfather rented at the airport.

The Aldens looked out the windows at the peaceful Wisconsin countryside. Rolling fields stretched for miles, broken only by big red barns and old stone houses. "Wow, there sure are a lot of cows around here," Benny noticed.

"Wisconsin is the land of the dairy cow," Grandfather told him. "As a matter of fact, there are more cows here than in any other state."

As Jessie admired a field of wildflowers, she thought of something. "Does Fran still make her own greeting cards?" she asked, remembering the beautiful card Grandfather had received on his birthday. It had been decorated with a border of pressed flowers.

Grandfather nodded. "Pressing flowers has always been a hobby of Fran's. A few years ago, after her husband died, she decided to turn her hobby into a small business. She put her greeting cards on display in a local gallery. Now they're selling like hotcakes."

"Wow, I guess Fran doesn't have to worry about money," Benny said.

"Her greeting card business helps pay the monthly bills," Grandfather replied, "but that's about all. Something always needs fixing in an old house, and it can be very costly. That's why Fran decided to take in a boarder for the summer — someone who pays to live with her. Her son wasn't very happy about it, but she needed the extra money."

"Why wasn't her son happy about it?" Henry wondered.

"From what I hear, Nelson thinks his mother is working too hard. And he's not happy that she spends most of her hard-earned money trying to keep the old house in shape. He doesn't see the point to it. The truth is, he's never shared his mother's fondness for the past. Now that he has a brand-new house of his own, he wants Fran to sell Shadowbox and move in with him."

"Sell Shadowbox?" cried Violet. "But that's Fran's home!"

"Oh, Fran's made it clear she has no intentions of selling," Grandfather assured Violet. "She loves Shadowbox too much for that. But it *has* caused some hard feelings between mother and son."

Before long, the Aldens were driving through the town of Cedarburg. Old cream-brick buildings lined both sides of the street. Tourists strolled along the sidewalks and in and out of the little shops.

In no time at all, they were pulling into a long driveway. At the end of the driveway was an old stone house nestled among the tall trees.

"Look, it's Shadowbox!" cried Benny.

"It sure is," said Grandfather, slowing to a stop. He waved to a tall, silver-haired lady rushing over to greet them. Everyone scrambled out of the car.

"It's good to see you, Fran!" Grandfather gave his friend a warm hug. "It's been too long between visits."

"You can say that again, James!" Fran's blue eyes were sparkling. "And these must be your wonderful grandchildren." The lace collar on her lilac dress fluttered in the breeze.

Grandfather smiled proudly as he introduced Henry, Jessie, Violet, and Benny. They all shook hands with Fran. "It's very nice to meet you," said Jessie, speaking for them all.

"Now I know why your house is called Shadowbox," Benny piped up. "It's shaped just like a big box, and it's hidden in the shadows of the trees."

"Exactly — yes!" said Fran, who seemed delighted that Benny had figured it out.

Benny grinned.

Glancing at his watch, Grandfather said, "I hate to rush off, but I have a dinner meeting to attend."

Fran waved that away. "You're here on business, James. I know that."

Grandfather lifted the suitcases from the car. "I should have everything wrapped up in a few days," he said, smiling at his friend. "Then we'll have time for a nice visit."

Fran smiled back. "I'll look forward to it."

The children waved good-bye to their grandfather, then they followed Fran into the house. As they set their suitcases down in the front hall, she turned to them. "Your grandfather tells me you're real experts at solving mysteries."

Benny beamed. "That's our specialty."

"We *have* solved quite a few," admitted Henry.

Fran was quiet for a moment, then she said, "The thing is, a mystery fell into my lap the other day. And I'm completely baffled by it."

"We'd love to help," offered Violet. And the others nodded eagerly.

Fran smiled gratefully. "I'll tell you about it after dinner," she promised. "But right now, it's time to introduce you to the runaway ghost."

The Aldens looked at one another in amazement. Were they about to meet a real ghost?

CHAPTER 2

The Ghostly Painting

Henry, Jessie, Violet, and Benny followed Fran into a cozy living room that looked out on Cedar Creek. Fresh flowers in colorful vases had been placed on every table. A sunny-yellow couch and buttercup-patterned chairs were grouped together invitingly around a large stone fireplace.

"What a pretty room," Jessie said admiringly.

"Thank you, Jessie," Fran smiled. "It's my favorite spot in the house."

"Oh, a painting of Shadowbox!" Violet said in surprise.

The other Aldens followed her gaze to the picture hanging above the fireplace. It was a peaceful summer scene with the stone house peeking out from among the trees. Nearby, a black-and-white cow grazed lazily in the late afternoon shadows.

"Meet the runaway ghost!" Fran gestured to the painting with a big sweep of her arm.

The Aldens looked at one another in confusion. Before they had a chance to ask any questions, Fran spoke again.

"It's wonderful, don't you think?" She sounded proud.

"It's a lovely painting," Jessie said, "but where's the runaway ghost?"

Henry added, "All I see is Shadowbox."

"Oh?" Fran lifted an eyebrow. "Perhaps there's something you're missing."

Henry looked again. "You can't mean . . . the cow?"

Nodding, Fran brushed a wisp of silver hair back from her face. "Her name was

Buttercup. But she's known as the runaway ghost."

The children were so surprised by Fran's words, they were speechless. Was the family ghost really a black-and-white cow? Jessie noticed a shiny brass plaque attached to the picture frame. Sure enough, the title of the painting was *The Runaway Ghost.*

"Buttercup's story begins many years ago," Fran said, making herself comfortable on the couch, "back when Shadowbox was still part of a big farm."

"This was once a farm?" Benny asked in surprise.

"Yes, indeed!" Fran told him. "My great-great-grandparents, Selden and Anne Gorton, started the farm back in the 1850s. They raised cows here for many, many years."

Benny looked puzzled. "What happened to it?" he wanted to know. "The farm, I mean."

"Selden and Anne's grandchildren decided not to be farmers. They sold off the land in bits and pieces. Now there's only Shadowbox and the lawns around it." A sad smile crossed Fran's face.

"Was Buttercup one of Selden and Anne's cows?" asked Jessie.

"As a matter of fact, she was the very first cow they ever owned," Fran replied.

Benny looked over at the painting. "Oh, I get it!" he said. "That's why the bell around her neck has the number one on it, right?"

"That's exactly right," Fran told him. "Selden and Anne were very fond of their black-and-white cow. She was more like a family pet than anything else. It's little wonder they were heartbroken when she disappeared."

"What . . . ?" Violet cried out in surprise. "How did Buttercup disappear?"

Fran shook her head sadly. "It happened in the winter of 1859."

The Aldens inched closer. They wanted to catch every word.

"One day, Buttercup wandered too far from the barn and she was caught in a blizzard. It was a terrible snowstorm. The poor thing couldn't find her way home," Fran said.

"Your ancestors went looking for her, didn't they?" Henry asked.

"Selden went out again and again, but the icy winds and the blinding snow kept driving him back. Finally, there was nothing left to do but wait out the storm. And by the time the snow stopped, it was too late."

Benny's eyes were huge. "Too late?"

"They never did find their treasured pet." Lowering her voice to a whisper, Fran added, "Buttercup had disappeared without a trace."

"How sad!" said Violet, who was taking a closer look at the painting of Buttercup.

Jessie came up behind her sister. "Well, at least Selden and Anne had a picture to — "

"Oh, my goodness, look!" Violet broke in as something caught her eye.

Curious, Henry joined his sisters by the fireplace. Benny was close behind.

"What's up?" Henry asked.

Violet pointed to the date next to the

artist's signature in a corner of the painting. "It's the strangest thing."

"Oh!" Jessie's eyebrows shot up when she saw the date. "This painting was made in 1866. But . . . Buttercup disappeared in 1859. Didn't she, Fran?"

"That's right, Jessie. A friend of my great-great grandparents painted that picture seven years *after* Buttercup disappeared."

"Was he painting from memory?" Violet asked.

Fran shook her head. "The artist had never been to Shadowbox until after the cow disappeared."

Benny gulped. "That's a . . . a painting of Buttercup's *ghost*?"

"Yes, it is, Benny," Fran said with a nod.

"How can that be?" Jessie couldn't believe it.

Henry added, "You don't really mean that, do you, Fran? You *can't* believe the artist painted a ghost."

"Maybe he painted a different cow," Violet offered as they sat down again. "Another black-and-white cow that looked a lot like Buttercup."

"But that doesn't explain the bell with the number one on it," Fran pointed out. "And there's something else," she added. "They say the artist was just putting the finishing touches on his painting when the black-and-white cow suddenly disappeared. It was almost as if . . ." She stopped midsentence.

"As if . . . what?" Benny asked in a whisper.

"As if the cow had vanished — just like that!" Fran said, with a snap of her fingers.

No one spoke for a moment. Then Henry said, "Has anyone else seen the runaway ghost?"

Fran smoothed down the collar of her dress. "In the old days, there were many sightings reported by family members. Sometimes visitors even heard the ghostly clanging of a cowbell late in the night. I've never heard it myself. I'm afraid I sleep much too soundly for that. It's been ages since the runaway ghost has been around."

Benny looked relieved.

As Fran turned her attention back to the painting, a funny look came over her face. "I've had the strangest feeling lately," she said, "that Buttercup's trying to tell me something."

The Aldens were startled. "Why do you say that, Fran?" Jessie wanted to know.

"Because of the mystery, Jessie," Fran explained. "I'm talking, of course, about the one that fell into my lap."

"Does the mystery have something to do with Buttercup?" Henry asked in surprise.

"That's one of the things I hope you'll figure out," Fran answered. Then she quickly changed the subject. "But now it's time for you to see the rest of the house."

As the Aldens followed Fran out of the room, Violet turned to look over her shoulder. She didn't really believe in ghosts, but she couldn't help wondering about that painting above the fireplace.

CHAPTER 3

Elephants and a Riddle

"Do you think it's true?" Benny asked his brother and sisters. He was standing at the window in the lace-and-lavender room that Violet and Jessie were sharing. The children had finished unpacking and were waiting for Violet to put more film in her camera.

Jessie, who was brushing her long brown hair, looked over at her younger brother. "What do you mean, Benny?"

Benny plopped down on Jessie's bed. "Do

you think Buttercup really *is* trying to tell Fran something?"

"No." Henry shook his head firmly. "Ghosts don't exist, Benny." But the youngest Alden didn't look convinced.

Violet looked up. "You must admit, Henry, it's awfully strange about that painting."

Benny was quick to agree. "How could the artist paint Buttercup's picture seven years after she disappeared?"

Henry shrugged. "That's a good question."

"I don't understand it, either," put in Jessie, as the four of them made their way downstairs. "But there must be a logical explanation for it."

"Like what?" demanded Benny.

None of them had an answer to that question.

"Something sure smells good!" Henry said, as they trooped into the kitchen.

Fran was humming to herself as she took the biscuits out of the oven. "I made my special meatballs in mushroom sauce." The table was already set for dinner, and she gestured for the children to sit down. "I'm hoping it'll hit the spot."

"Grandfather told us you're a great cook, Fran," Jessie said, taking a seat next to Benny.

"Oh, I just follow the old family recipes, Jessie," Fran said. "Selden's wife, Anne, brought most of them with her from St. Ives."

"St. Ives?" said Henry.

"That was the name of Anne's hometown in England." Fran set a dish of mashed potatoes on the table.

"It must've been hard for Anne to leave her hometown," Violet said. Violet was shy, and meeting new people often made her nervous.

Fran pulled up a chair. "I imagine Anne *was* homesick at first, but she loved Selden, and she never regretted her new life in Wisconsin."

Just then, a voice behind them made the children turn around quickly in surprise.

"Sorry I'm late." A slim young woman

came rushing into the room. She was dressed in a sleeveless blouse and a brightly-flowered skirt. Her blond hair was pulled back into a ponytail.

Fran smiled warmly. "We only just sat down, Lottie." She quickly introduced the Aldens to her boarder, Lottie Brighton.

"A newlywed couple came into the gallery just as I was leaving," Lottie explained, after saying hello to everyone. "They were eager for a sketch." She slipped into the empty seat beside Henry. "What could I do? I needed the extra money."

Seeing the children's slightly puzzled faces, Fran said, "Lottie has a job at one of the local galleries in Cedarburg. She draws sketches of the tourists who come to town."

That sounded like fun to Violet. "Oh, you must love going to work every day, Lottie!" Violet liked to sketch and draw, and she was good at it, too.

Lottie placed a napkin over her lap. "Yes, I *do* enjoy it, and it's good practice," she said. "I just wish it paid more."

"Lottie's putting herself through art school," Fran explained.

"At the rate I'm going, I'll never have enough money for the fall term." Lottie frowned as she put green beans on her plate.

"I know what it's like to be on a tight budget, Lottie." Fran placed a comforting hand on the young woman's arm. "It isn't easy, but you'll find a way."

"Grandfather always says, 'Where there's a will, there's a way,'" Benny said, then went back to wolfing down meatballs.

Lottie nodded. "Yes, sometimes you have to do whatever it takes," she said, "even if . . ." Her words trailed away in a sigh.

Henry watched her expectantly, but Lottie didn't finish the sentence.

Just after Benny had eaten the last meatball, there was a soft tapping on the kitchen door. Wiping her mouth with a napkin, Fran hurried to answer it.

A suntanned woman with a cheery smile was standing on the doorstep. She was dressed in a T-shirt and shorts, and her thick dark curls were held back from her face with a white headband. At her elbow was a girl about Violet's age, holding a pie.

"Well, look who's here!" Fran stepped aside to usher in the new arrivals. Then she introduced everyone to her neighbors, Cora Roback and her daughter, Reese.

"We made a special welcome-to-Cedarburg dessert," Reese said, smiling over at the Aldens. "Ghost pie!" She held it up.

Benny's mouth dropped open. "Did you say *ghost* pie?"

"Don't worry, Benny." Cora laughed. "It's really just plain old apple pie."

"But guess what?" added Reese, who had the same dark hair and big brown eyes as her mother. "It's so delicious that it disappears — just like that!" She snapped her fingers exactly as Fran had done. "That's why we call it — "

"Ghost pie!" everyone cried out.

"What a perfect way to end our meal!"

Fran said as she set the pie on the counter.

Jessie gave Reese a friendly smile. "I'm glad I left room for dessert."

"The meatballs hit the spot," put in Benny, "but I've still got a *big* spot left for ghost pie."

"Count me in, too," added Henry. Violet nodded.

"Cora owns an antique store in town," Fran informed the Aldens. "She also writes articles for a local magazine. Right now, she's working on one about Shadowbox and the other old homes of Cedarburg."

"Oh!" Henry said. "I can't wait to read all about the runaway ghost."

"Oh, yes!" Fran rubbed her hands together with pleasure. "The family ghost will get quite a write-up, I'm sure. I mean, how can it miss?"

Jessie couldn't help noticing that Cora shifted uncomfortably.

"The problem is — " Cora began to say. But Fran interrupted.

"If you need more information, Cora, just

let me know. I'll fill you in on all the ghostly details."

Cora held up a hand. "You might as well know, Fran," she told her, "I decided not to mention the runaway ghost in the article."

"What was that?" There was a look of shock on Fran's face.

"Well, there haven't been any sightings in years, right? And even the ones from long ago were probably staged — you know, to entertain the guests. The whole idea of a ghost cow seems a bit . . . far-fetched. Don't you think?" Cora suddenly seemed unable to look Fran in the eye.

"Far-fetched?" Fran stiffened.

Lottie offered an opinion. "I agree with Cora. An article like that should stick to the facts."

Cora nodded. "Exactly!" she said. "The facts and nothing *but* the facts."

"People would laugh if you mentioned a ghost cow," added Lottie. "You mustn't even consider such a thing, Cora."

Jessie caught Henry's eye. Why was Lot-

tie butting in? The article had nothing to
do with her.

"I want this article to be taken seriously,"
Cora added.

"I see." Fran looked as if she wanted to
argue, but she didn't.

Violet didn't like to see the disappointment on Fran's face. She just had to say
something. "But . . . the runaway ghost is
a part of the history of Shadowbox. That
story goes all the way back to the 1850s!"

Reese turned to her mother. "Violet's
right. You can't write about Shadowbox and
not mention the runaway ghost. They go
together like . . . like ghost pie and ice
cream!"

Cora frowned. "Reese, please!" She gave
her daughter a warning look. "You're not
helping matters."

"I'm sure you know best, Cora," Fran
said, forcing a smile. "No reason for anyone to be upset." But it was plain that Fran
was upset.

"Sure nice to meet everyone!" Cora was
already steering her daughter toward the

door. She suddenly seemed eager to get away. "See you later."

As the door closed behind them, Fran mumbled, "If Cora thinks I'm going to sit back and do nothing, she should think again. I mean, really!"

The Aldens exchanged worried looks. What was Fran planning to do?

"Now," said Fran, who was back to her cheery self, "are you ready to hear about that mystery?"

The Aldens nodded eagerly. They were sitting in the living room, sipping apple cider and eating ghost pie and ice cream.

"All the clues are right here," Fran said. She reached for a small wooden box on the table beside her. "But, for the life of me, I can't make head nor tails of any of it."

"We'll do our best to help," Henry promised.

"We're good detectives," added Benny.

"Detectives?" echoed Lottie.

"These children have a real knack for tracking down clues," Fran told her.

"They've offered to help me solve a mystery."

"Oh?" Lottie raised her eyebrows.

"Yes, indeed. The mystery fell into my lap a few weeks ago, when I was having repairs done in the front hall. Some of the floorboards were warped and needed replacing." Fran looked around at each of the Aldens. "One of the workmen found this under a loose floorboard." She gave the mysterious box a little shake.

Violet knelt down beside Fran's chair to get a closer look. "Oh, the box is decorated with pressed flowers."

"Yes, it's quite lovely, really," Fran responded. "And very old, too. I would guess that it's been hidden away for a long time."

Jessie looked questioningly at her. "What makes you say that, Fran?"

"Take a good look at the box, Jessie. See how faded the flowers are? Time takes its toll on pressed flowers, I'm afraid. The colors eventually fade."

"That's good detective work," praised Henry.

Violet ran her fingers gently over the box. A little shiver went down her spine as she made a discovery. "The flowers are buttercups!"

The others gathered round to check it out. Sure enough, the entire box was covered with nothing but buttercups.

"Is that why you think the mystery has something to do with the runaway ghost?" Henry asked Fran.

Nodding her head, Fran said, "There must be some kind of connection. I can feel it in my bones."

"But what's *inside* the box?" Benny asked, his mouth full of ghost pie. He could hardly stand the suspense.

With a quick motion, Fran flipped open the lid and removed a single sheet of paper, yellowed with age. "There's a riddle inside," she said. "And a rather strange one at that!" Putting on her reading glasses, Fran began to read aloud:

"The thing you hold
Is the thing you seek,

A treasure waits,
Shadows speak.

Solve this riddle,
And you will see,
You're ready to solve,
Riddle three."

The Aldens stared wide-eyed at Fran. Then Benny said, "Riddle three?" He looked confused.

"I guess there was once a riddle one that led to the secret hiding place under the floorboards," Fran said.

"Well, one thing's for sure," said Jessie, "nobody ever figured it out."

"What makes you say that, Jessie?" Benny asked.

"Because the box was still in its hiding place, Benny," she explained.

"Oh, right!" Benny said.

"Just think," put in Fran, "if I hadn't decided to spiff up the front hall, the box would still be there."

Benny was deep in thought. "But shadows can't speak, can they?" he asked, his mind still on the riddle.

Shaking his head, Henry said, "I've never heard of it."

Fran leaned close, as though about to share a secret. "It might have something to do with the elephants."

"Elephants?" Benny almost choked on his pie. "*What* elephants?"

Fran reached into the box again and pulled out a handful of elephants cut from black paper. "There's a whole herd of these . . . these shadow elephants inside," she said, as if not knowing what else to call them.

"Hey, that makes it a shadowbox!" Benny realized.

Fran laughed a little. "Yes, I suppose it *is* a kind of shadowbox."

Everyone had a turn inspecting the contents of the box. After thumbing through the shadow elephants once . . . twice . . . three times, Henry drew his eyebrows together in a frown.

"I don't get it," he said. "What do these elephants have to do with the riddle?"

The other Aldens crowded around to take another look.

"Each of the elephants looks different, but their trunks all point up," Jessie noticed. "Do you think that could mean anything?"

"You're right, Jessie, they're all like that," Henry said with a nod.

"But why are their trunks pointing up?" Benny wanted to know. "And what does the riddle mean?"

Henry scratched behind his neck. "Beats me!"

"What'd I tell you?" said Fran. "It doesn't make sense, does it?" She took a sip of her apple cider.

The Aldens sat in puzzled silence. They had never come across a mystery like this one before. If shadows did talk, then what would the shadow elephants want to tell them?

Lottie spoke up. "If you ask me, it doesn't mean anything. It's probably just a game of some kind," she said matter-of-factly. "That box has probably been hidden away since the Victorian era. Weren't parlor games popular back then?"

Benny wrinkled up his forehead. "What's the Victorian era?"

"The olden days," explained Henry. "Before computers or television."

"They didn't have electricity back then," added Jessie.

Lottie nodded. "That's right. In the evenings, they'd read or sew or play games. This easily could be part of a game."

Fran had to admit it was possible. "My great-great-grandmother Anne *was* a very creative person. She loved coming up with games to keep her children amused."

Benny's face fell. "You mean, there might not be a treasure waiting?"

"Maybe not," said Jessie. "But we won't know for sure until we do some investigating."

"Why get yourselves all worked up about nothing?" insisted Lottie. "If there ever was a treasure, it must be long gone."

Henry and Jessie exchanged glances.

Why was Lottie so sure there wasn't a treasure?

Before they had a chance to ask any questions, Lottie suddenly got to her feet. "Well, I think I'll go up to my room and paint for a while," she said.

"Oh, what are you painting, Lottie?" Violet asked.

Lottie shrugged a little. "Nothing special," she said.

Fran chuckled. "Lottie's very hush-hush about her art. I haven't been able to get a word out of her."

"Oh," Benny said, disappointed. "So we can't see it?"

Lottie shook her head firmly and went upstairs.

Violet couldn't help wondering why Fran's boarder was being so secretive.

CHAPTER 4

Moooo!

Clang, clang. Clang, clang, clang.
Violet blinked and sat up in bed. It was the middle of the night. The house was dark and quiet. What had awakened her?

"Jessie?" she whispered, rubbing her arms to warm them.

Jessie didn't answer. She was sleeping soundly.

Violet slid out of bed and padded across the room. She looked through the window down on the moonlit garden. Everything was still. The only sound was of crickets singing.

"Violet?" Jessie began to stir. "Is something wrong?"

"I . . . I thought I heard something," Violet said.

"Like what?" Jessie asked drowsily.

"A clanging sound," Violet whispered, "like a bell ringing."

Jessie yawned. "It was probably just a dream."

"Yes, I'm sure you're right," Violet said as she climbed back into bed. But there was a part of her that wasn't sure at all.

The next morning, after a big breakfast of scrambled eggs, sausages, fresh fruit, and cinnamon toast, the Aldens set off with Fran for a walking tour of Cedarburg. Violet brought her camera along to take snapshots of the old mills that stood on the banks of Cedar Creek. As they walked through town, they stopped here and there to browse in several of the interesting little shops.

"This must be Cora's store," Henry said, tilting his head back to see the sign above one of the shops. The bright blue letters spelled ROBACK'S ANTIQUE SHOP.

"It sure is," Fran said. "And it's a great place to go treasure hunting."

"*Treasure* hunting?" Benny looked surprised.

"Treasures from the past, Benny," Fran explained. "Come and see."

As the Aldens stepped inside, their gaze took in all the old-fashioned picture frames, coal-oil lamps, braided rugs, stiff-backed chairs, and dusty old books that filled the shop. Every nook and cranny was overflowing with antiques.

"These old treasures have seen better days," Fran told them. "Every little scratch and scuff mark is a clue about the past."

"Fran!" Cora walked toward them, looking surprised. "I'm glad you stopped by."

Fran smiled a little. "Did you think I'd stay away?" she asked.

"I thought you might still be upset," Cora said. She bit her lip nervously. "I sure hope there are no hard feelings about that article. I wouldn't want it to come between us."

"Don't worry, I've forgotten all about it," Fran replied — a bit stiffly, Jessie thought.

Cora let out a long breath. "That's a load off my mind." She noticed someone waiting by the counter and hurried away.

Fran went over to check out a basket of wooden clothes pins. Henry and Jessie walked over to the stamp collections. Benny dug deep into a bin of old cookie cutters. And Violet looked at some antique box cameras.

A short while later, Benny held up a cookie cutter shaped like a cow. "Look!" He tugged on Violet's arm. "Do we have enough money to get this for Mrs. McGregor?" Mrs. McGregor was the Aldens' housekeeper, and an excellent cook.

Violet counted her change. "Good idea, Benny. Looks like we have enough."

As they waited in line, Benny said, "Now Mrs. McGregor can make ghost cookies — the kind that disappear just like that!" He snapped his fingers.

Violet laughed. "Oh, Benny! Mrs. McGregor's cookies always disappear when you're around."

As they stepped up to the counter, Cora gave them a big smile. "Found something, did you?"

Benny nodded. "A ghost cookie cutter."

"Well, now, that *is* quite a find." Cora chuckled as she took the money that Violet handed her.

"It's a present for Mrs. McGregor," Benny added. "She makes the best cookies in the world! Right, Violet?"

But Violet didn't answer. Something had caught her attention.

Benny followed his sister's gaze to a dented old bell hanging on the side of the counter. "Hey, that's just like Buttercup's bell!" he said. "Except, Buttercup's had the number one on it."

"That old cowbell's quite beaten up," Cora said, as she slipped the cookie cutter into a bag. "But it still rings. Go ahead and give it a try."

Violet picked up the bell. She was surprised at how heavy it was.

Clang, clang. Clang, clang, clang.

She recognized that sound! It was the same clanging she'd heard in the middle of the night! *Is it possible the runaway ghost has returned?* Violet wondered. Then she had a thought. "Do stray cows ever wander into town?" she asked Cora.

"Never heard of it." Cora shook her head.

Violet had little time to think about it. They were soon waving good-bye and filing out the door.

Fran looked at her wristwatch. "It's almost lunchtime," she said. "There's a restaurant just down the street. Why don't you go on ahead and get a table for us? I want to pop in to see my son for a moment." She nodded toward the Cedarburg Insurance office across the street. "We had a silly squabble recently, and I'd like to patch things up." With a little wave, she hurried off.

The Aldens headed toward the restaurant. They'd passed a bookstore and a pottery shop when Jessie stopped. She peered through the big plate-glass window of a gallery. "Oh, look," she said. "There's Lottie. This must be the gallery where she works."

They all looked through the window. Sure enough, Lottie was sitting at a small table in a corner of the gallery, talking to a man the Aldens didn't recognize. While Lottie talked, the man tapped his chin thoughtfully. He had broad shoulders and a beard, and his dark hair was slicked back.

Benny was about to rap on the window to get Lottie's attention, but Jessie stopped him. "Hold on, Benny," she said. "I don't think we should bother her while she's working." With that, they set off again.

After settling into a table on the restaurant's patio, the Aldens watched the tourists coming and going along the sidewalk. Then they turned their attention to Fran's mystery.

"I don't get it," said Benny, scratching his head.

"What don't you get?" asked Jessie.

Benny looked around at them. "The riddle says, *'The thing you hold/Is the thing you seek.'*" A frown crossed his round face. "Why should we look for something if we've already got it?"

Jessie had a thought. "I bet we're supposed to look for more shadow elephants."

"Or maybe we're supposed to look for another shadowbox," Violet offered. "Like the one with the elephants in it."

"I have a hunch we should figure out why their trunks are pointing up," insisted Henry, thinking that was some kind of clue.

"You might be right, Henry," Jessie told him. "But that's a tough one to figure out."

Henry couldn't argue. "It's a mystery, that's for sure," he said.

"I just hope Lottie's wrong about the treasure," Benny added as the waitress brought the menus. "She says it's long gone."

"What I can't figure out," said Jessie, "is how she can be so sure."

"Maybe she just wants us to *believe* there isn't a treasure," suggested Benny.

"But . . . why?" asked Violet.

"So that she can find it herself." Benny looked around at his brother and sisters. "She needs money for school, remember?"

Just then they noticed Fran coming down the street. She appeared to be having a heated talk with a tall, sandy-haired man in a business suit. The Aldens didn't mean to eavesdrop, but they couldn't help overhearing what they were saying as they drew closer.

"I'm quite capable of making my own decisions," Fran told the man. "Why can't you respect my choices?"

The man was shaking his head. "You never have two pennies to rub together as it is! How can you keep pouring money into that old house?" He sounded annoyed.

"That old house is my home," Fran said crossly. "And *that* means more to me than all the money in the world!"

"I can see I'm wasting my breath,

Mother!" The sandy-haired man threw up his hands and stormed away.

"Wow," said Benny, keeping his voice low. "That must be Fran's son."

"I guess they didn't patch things up after all," Violet said with a sigh.

"Just wait till we find the treasure," added Benny. "Fran will have *lots* of pennies to rub together then!"

"I hope so, Benny," said Henry. "I hope so."

As Fran stepped onto the patio, she spotted the children immediately and walked over. She smiled as she pulled up a chair, but it wasn't much of a smile. "Sure feels good to take a load off my feet," she said with a sigh.

Henry could see that the argument with her son had upset Fran. He was trying to think of something cheery to say, when Jessie spoke up.

"Cedarburg is a beautiful town," she remarked. "No wonder you love living here, Fran."

"I can't imagine living anywhere else, Jessie." Fran let out another sigh.

They were all quiet for a while as they studied the menus. When the waitress came back to the table, Fran ordered a cheese sandwich and an iced tea. Henry chose fish and chips, and orange juice. Jessie and Violet both ordered corned beef sandwiches, cole slaw, and milk. Benny decided on a hamburger, French fries, and chocolate milk.

"Tell us more about the artist who painted the runaway ghost," Violet said, turning to Fran. "Did he ever become famous?"

Fran laughed. "Oh, no. I'm afraid that painting isn't worth much to anyone but me. The artist was a friend of Selden and Anne's. His name was Homer and that's about all we know about him. I don't even know what his last name was!"

"How do you know his first name?" Benny asked.

"Well, he signed it on the painting," Fran

replied, "and my great-great-grandfather mentioned him a lot in the diary he kept. They were very close. So many of the entries say, 'Homer and Anne and I did this and, Homer and Anne and I did that.' They had great fun together!"

"Well, he was a wonderful artist," Jessie said.

"You know, there's an old photograph of Homer around somewhere," Fran informed them. "He's standing with Selden and Anne on the front lawn of Shadowbox. They're all holding croquet mallets."

"What's a croquet mallet?" Benny wanted to know.

"It's for croquet, an old-fashioned game, Benny," explained Henry. "The mallets are used to hit wooden balls through little arches called wickets."

Benny grinned. "Sounds like fun."

Fran smiled at the youngest Alden. "As I recall, there's an old croquet set up in the attic. If you don't mind rummaging around for it, you're welcome to give it a try."

The Aldens didn't mind at all. As soon as

they got back to Shadowbox, they hurried up to the attic. "Whew!" said Benny. "It sure is hot up here."

Henry nodded. "Like an oven," he said as he glanced around at the clutter of dusty books, cardboard boxes, broken toys, and lumpy old chairs.

"Let's split up," Jessie suggested in her practical way. "Then it won't take so long."

Benny sat down to poke around in a box of comic books and jigsaw puzzles. Henry opened the drawers of a dusty old dresser. Jessie sorted through a hamper filled with odds and ends. And Violet searched in a trunk covered with faded stickers from far-away places.

It wasn't long before Benny let out a cheer. "I found it!" he said, holding open the lid of a wooden box. "At least, I think I did."

Henry went over to take a look. "Way to go, Benny!" he said, glancing down at the box filled with mallets and balls and wickets.

"Omigosh!" Violet was still standing over the old trunk, her eyes wide.

"Is anything wrong?" Jessie asked her sister.

Violet stammered, "It's a . . . a *trunk!*"

Jessie, Henry, and Benny looked from Violet to the trunk and back again. They seemed puzzled.

"What's strange about that, Violet?" Benny wanted to know. "Lots of attics have old trunks in them."

"But . . . it's a *trunk* and it's *up* in the attic!" Violet sounded excited.

Henry suddenly understood. "The elephants' trunks were pointing up!"

"Now that you mention it," said Jessie, "a trunk can be an elephant's long nose — "

"Or it can be a big chest for storing things," finished Violet.

"The thing you hold/ Is the thing you seek!" cried Benny. "We were supposed to seek another trunk! That's where the next clue must be."

"Got to be," agreed Henry.

Violet, Benny, Henry, and Jessie searched carefully through the trunk. It was filled with old-fashioned clothes that smelled of mothballs. But when they were finished, all they'd found was an envelope bulging with old photographs. Jessie tucked the envelope into her back pocket to show Fran.

"Looks like we struck out," Violet was forced to admit.

"I don't get it." Jessie looked down at the trunk. "According to the clues, this should be the spot."

"Then where's the next riddle?" Benny wanted to know.

The Aldens looked at one another. How were they ever going to solve such a strange mystery?

CHAPTER 5

A Pile of Rubbish?

The Aldens found Fran sitting in her workroom, a basket of flowers in front of her. Newspapers had been spread over a long table, and there was a thick phone book nearby. When Jessie tugged the old photographs from her pocket, Fran's face broke into a smile.

"Well, you've made my day, Jessie. I knew I'd put these pictures somewhere for safe-keeping, but I'd forgotten exactly where." She slipped the envelope into her apron pocket with a happy sigh.

"And I found the old croquet set," Benny reminded everyone.

Fran turned to him with a warm smile. "That was very helpful, too, Benny."

The Aldens glanced around the sunny workroom. Metal file cabinets lined one wall. Wooden shelves filled with neatly-labeled shoe boxes stood against another wall. By the curtained window, there was a large desk cluttered with papers. In the corner, half hidden by a potted plant, phone books were piled high.

"I've never seen so many phone books!" Benny's eyes were wide.

Fran threw her head back and laughed. "Folks in town save them for me, Benny. The pages are perfect for pressing flowers. They soak up all the moisture." She looked around at the Aldens. "Anybody interested in pressing flowers? I'd be happy to show you how."

"Oh, yes!" said Violet, her eyes shining. The others nodded eagerly.

Fran handed out wicker baskets. "For starters, you'll need to gather some flowers," she said. "If you see anything in the garden that strikes your fancy, just help yourselves. Oh, and don't forget about wildflowers," she added. "Even weeds have charm."

"I think I'll pick buttercups," Benny decided as they headed for the door. "They're my favorites."

Outside, Jessie and Henry followed the stepping-stone path through the garden, while Violet and Benny searched for wildflowers on the banks of the creek. Their baskets were soon bursting with summer colors. Fran nodded approvingly when they came back into the room.

"That's the ticket!" she said. "You've got a real mix of colors there."

The Aldens sat down at the table. Fran showed them how to spread the flowers out on the newspapers, then carefully place them, spaced apart, on the pages of a phone book.

After they'd been working for a while, Benny looked up. "This is so cool," he said.

Henry agreed. He was holding a morn-

ing glory under Fran's magnifying glass. "The flowers are all so different."

"That's true, Henry," Fran said. "As Reese would say, there are no boring bits. Every leaf and tendril is special."

"Oh, does Reese press flowers, too?" Violet asked.

"Yes, I've been teaching her everything I know." Fran's lips curled up in a smile. "She really is the dearest child."

Jessie was wondering about something. "How did you get started, Fran? Pressing flowers, I mean."

"It's a family tradition, Jessie." Fran gestured to the framed verses hanging along the back wall. "Those were my great-great-grandmother Anne's creations. She didn't write the verses, but she decorated each one with a border of pressed flowers. Anne loved making everything beautiful. Apparently she even painted buttercups all over the walls of the old mudroom."

"The old mudroom?" Jessie gave Fran a questioning look.

"It used to be just off the kitchen," Fran

explained. "A place for dirty boots and coats. After Anne decorated it, everybody called it the Buttercup Room. But it was torn down long before my time."

Jessie glanced at Henry. If Anne pressed flowers, wasn't it possible she'd decorated that mysterious box? It was clear she loved buttercups. Was Lottie right? Was it all just a parlor game? That would explain why they hadn't found any clues in the trunk. They were probably long gone — just like the treasure.

Violet, who was taking a closer look at the framed verses on the wall, suddenly turned around. "There's one called *A Little St. Ives Rhyme.*"

"Anne was very fond of her hometown, Violet," Fran said. "She even named the old tree house *Little St. Ives.*"

That got Benny's attention. "Tree house?"

"Selden built it for his sons," Fran explained. "But the tree was struck by lightning long ago. The tree house was destroyed."

"Oh, that's sad," said Benny.

Fran nodded. "We get some terrible thunderstorms here in Wisconsin."

They all bent to their work again. A short while later, Benny placed his last flower in the phone book he was sharing with Violet. "So, is that it?" he asked Fran.

"Not quite, Benny. The flowers need heavy weights pressing down on them." Fran walked over to the closet. She threw open the door to reveal stacks of bricks. "I find these work quite nicely."

Following Fran's instructions, Henry stacked the phone books on the floor of the closet, then placed the bricks on top.

"Nice job, Henry," Fran praised. "The flowers take a few months to dry. But I've got a ton of them already pressed. If you're interested in making your own greeting cards later, you're welcome to use whatever flowers you want."

Violet's eyes lit up. "Really?"

Fran winked. "I don't see why not."

Violet was thrilled. She clapped her hands together excitedly.

Jessie said, "Thanks so much for the lesson, Fran." The others thanked her too.

"If you keep at it, you'll get the hang of it soon enough." Fran glanced at her watch. "I guess I'd better get a move on. My chores are waiting."

When she was gone, the Aldens set to work cleaning up. They were just finishing when they noticed someone standing in the doorway. A tall, sandy-haired man, his suit jacket over his arm, was watching them through narrowed eyes.

"Who are you?" he demanded. "And how'd you get in here?"

The children were so surprised by his harsh tone, they were speechless. Finally, Henry recovered his voice. "You must be Fran's son, Nelson," he said with a friendly smile. "We're the Aldens. I'm Henry. This is my brother, Benny, and my sisters, Violet and Jessie."

"Fran invited us to stay with her for a few days," added Jessie. "She's a friend of our grandfather's."

Shaking his head, Nelson muttered, "Might as well add a revolving door out front with so many people staying here." He sounded annoyed.

"But we're here to help," Benny protested. "We're going to solve a mystery and find a treasure for Fran."

Nelson did not look happy to hear this. "Give me a break! My mother told me all about the riddle she found. Don't worry, there's no treasure. That mystery is just a pile of rubbish."

"Fran doesn't think it's rubbish," Jessie said quietly.

Nelson cut in, "Just don't get my mother's hopes up for nothing." He shifted his suit jacket impatiently from one arm to the other. "She works so hard, she never has time for me anymore. We used to have good times together. We used to — " He stopped abruptly as if realizing he'd said too much. "I just want her life to be a bit easier. What's wrong with that?"

"Maybe Fran wants a happy life," Violet offered, "not an easy one."

Nelson opened his mouth as if about to speak, then closed it again. He wheeled around and hurried away.

Henry shook his head in astonishment. "Nelson sure thinks he knows best."

A few minutes later, Fran poked her head into the room. "I thought I heard Nelson's voice. Is he here?"

Henry said, "He left already."

"I don't think he likes us very much," added Benny.

"Oh, you mustn't think that," said Fran. "Nelson's a good man, but he places too much importance on money. Ever since his father died, he's been worrying about me because I'm on a tight budget. He doesn't seem to realize I can take care of myself."

"Maybe he just wants to be a part of your life," Violet suggested, softening a little toward Nelson.

Fran looked at Violet in surprise. Then she quickly changed the subject. "Any thoughts on the mystery riddle?"

"We were pretty sure we had a lead," said Henry. "But it fizzled out."

"Oh!" Fran looked disappointed.

"Don't worry," Benny said. "We'll get to the bottom of it."

Jessie didn't say anything. She couldn't help wondering if Nelson was right. Were they getting Fran's hopes up for nothing?

CHAPTER 6

The Tree House

During dinner that night, Fran and the Aldens did most of the talking. Lottie was strangely quiet.

"When I'm making my designs, I keep a bowl nearby filled with pressed flowers," Fran was telling them. "And some ribbons, too, of course — satin, velvet, and a few snippets of lace."

Violet swallowed her last bite of chicken. "That must be the hard part," she guessed. "Coming up with a good design, I mean."

"Well, the secret is to have something in

67

mind before you begin." Fran took a sip of water. "But you really can't go wrong. Flowers always look nice."

As Henry and Jessie stood to clear the dishes, Fran said, "You're not yourself tonight, Lottie. Is anything wrong?"

The young woman's face reddened. "Oh, no, nothing's wrong." She got up from the table. "I think I'll skip dessert if you don't mind."

Benny's jaw dropped. "But . . . we're having strawberry shortcake!"

"Yes, and I'm sure it's delicious," Lottie said, smiling a little for the first time. "But I'd much rather paint right now."

"It must be very hard, Lottie," Jessie said, "making that kind of switch."

Lottie's whole face suddenly changed. Her smile faded and her eyes narrowed. She looked like a different person. "And what's that supposed to mean?" she asked in a strained voice. "Are you implying that — "

Jessie felt her cheeks turning pink. "I . . . I only meant that it must be hard switching from sketching to painting every day."

Lottie was clearly startled. "Oh, I didn't realize . . ." She quickly left the room without finishing her sentence.

"What was that all about?" Henry wondered.

"You got me!" Jessie answered. "Lottie's awfully touchy."

"Well, there's no need for anyone else to skip dessert," Fran said, as she dished up the strawberry shortcake.

Benny was glad to hear that.

After feasting on Fran's wonderful dessert, the Aldens washed and dried the dishes. Then they went outside to play croquet. Jessie was helping Henry set up the wickets when she noticed Reese watching from a distance.

"Hi, Reese!" she called out to her.

Reese walked over and gave the Aldens a big smile.

"We're learning how to play croquet," Violet told her cheerfully.

"You can play with us if you want," offered Benny. "Those arches are called, um . . ."

"Wickets," Henry reminded him.

"Right," said Benny. "And you hit the ball through them."

"Sounds like fun," Reese said as Violet handed her a mallet.

They were soon laughing and cheering as they hit the wooden balls through the wickets. Sometimes they hit a ball too hard and had to go searching for it in the long grass by the creek. But they didn't mind. It was a beautiful evening and the birds were singing. It wasn't until the shadows grew longer that they finally put the game away.

"Guess what, Reese?" Benny said, as they all sat together on the kitchen steps.

"What, Benny?" Reese replied.

"We went to your mother's antique shop today," he told her, "and I bought a cookie cutter shaped like a ghost cow."

"Oh, Benny!" Jessie laughed. "It's not shaped like a ghost cow. It's in the shape of an ordinary cow."

Reese was quiet for a moment. "I keep thinking about that magazine article," she said. "My mother says Fran will get over it. But I'm not so sure."

Henry looked at her questioningly. "You mean because the runaway ghost will be left out?"

Reese nodded. "I told my mother it isn't right. The story of Buttercup means a whole lot to Fran."

"Your mother seemed pretty firm about it," said Jessie.

Violet agreed. "I don't think she's going to change her mind."

"No, she hasn't budged," admitted Reese. "Not yet, anyway," she added with a mysterious little smile. "Well, I have to be going. Thanks for the game!" With that, she was on her feet and sprinting home across the grass.

"That's a bit strange, don't you think?" remarked Jessie. "Why does Reese think her mother will change her mind?"

Henry shrugged. "Maybe it's just wishful thinking. But I hope she's right."

The Aldens went back into the house. After pouring lemonade into tall glasses, they headed for the living room. Fran was sorting through the old photographs from the attic with Lottie.

"So, what's the verdict?" Fran looked up and smiled as the children walked into the room. "Did you enjoy croquet?"

"We sure did," Henry answered. "Reese even played for a while." He sank down in a buttercup-patterned chair.

"I was hoping you'd spend time together." Fran seemed pleased. "Speaking of croquet," she added, waving a photograph in the air, "I thought you might like to see that picture of Homer." She held it out to Violet. "I was ever so pleased to find it with the other photos. It's the only one we have."

Violet studied the photograph that Fran handed her. It was faded with age and badly creased in places. But it still provided a glimpse of two young men in jackets and trousers. They were standing on either side of a young woman in a hat and a long dress.

Benny checked it out over Violet's shoulder. "Look, they *are* holding mallets."

Fran nodded. "Selden's the young man

with the mustache and the straw hat, and that's Anne standing beside him." She pointed. "Homer's on the far right. He's the one with the flower in his buttonhole."

Fran waved another photograph in the air. "Here's another one you might find interesting. I'd forgotten we even had a picture of the old tree house."

Benny's face lit up. "You mean, the one Anne called Little St. Ives?"

Nodding, Fran handed the photo to Benny. "It's just peeking out from the branches of the tree. Can you spot it there?"

The other Aldens gathered around. "I can see Little St. Ives!" cried Benny. "Wow, too bad it was struck by lightning."

Just then, Lottie stood up. "I think I'll hit the sack early tonight," she said. "It's been a long day." She stretched and yawned.

"I believe I'll do the same," added Fran, removing her reading glasses. She placed the envelope of photographs on the table beside her. "That walk around Cedarburg left me tuckered out." She said good night, then followed Lottie out of the room.

Benny rubbed his eyes and yawned.

Smiling over at her little brother, Jessie said, "Early to bed sounds like a good idea."

As they started for the door, Violet noticed that Henry hung back. His eyes were still glued to the photograph of the tree house.

"What is it, Henry?" she asked. "What's wrong?"

Henry didn't answer. Instead, he dashed out of the room. He returned a few moments later with Fran's magnifying glass. "I think I see something in this photograph," he said, examining it closely. He had noticed something the others hadn't.

Jessie glanced over Henry's shoulder. "I don't understand. It's just a picture of a tree house."

"That's what I thought, too," said Henry. "Then I noticed something carved into the tree."

Jessie studied the picture through the

magnifying glass. "You're right, Henry. There *is* something carved into the tree."

"What is it?" Benny wanted to know.

"An arrow," Jessie answered. She looked from the photograph to Henry and back again. "But what does it mean?"

"The arrow's pointing *up*," Henry said. "And it's — "

Jessie drew in her breath. "And it's carved into the *trunk* of the tree!" she said, finishing Henry's sentence.

Violet and Benny stared at Jessie. They looked totally confused.

"The clues weren't leading us to that trunk in the attic at all," Henry concluded, a smile spreading across his face.

Jessie agreed. "They were leading us straight to the old tree house."

"So is that the answer to the riddle?" Benny was getting more excited by the second. "Is the answer a tree house?"

"I'm sure of it." Henry nodded. "Remember what you called the box Fran found?"

"A shadowbox," Benny said. "Because it's filled with shadow elephants."

Henry nodded. Then he began to recite, *"The thing you hold/ Is the thing you seek."* He looked over at his brother and sisters. "Violet was right. The riddle was telling us to seek another shadowbox."

Jessie settled into a chair. "That makes sense. The tree house *is* shaped like a box. And it's half hidden in the shadows of the tree."

"So it's a shadowbox, too!" cried Benny. "We were holding a shadowbox, and we were supposed to look for a shadowbox." The youngest Alden did a little dance. Figuring out clues was always fun.

Jessie sank back against a cushion. "There's only one problem."

Violet looked over at her. "What's that?"

"We'll never find the third riddle." Jessie sounded very sure.

"Why not, Jessie?" Benny asked her.

"Remember, Benny?" she said. "The tree house was destroyed."

"Ouch!" Henry winced. "You're right, Jessie. If the third riddle was hidden somewhere inside the tree house, it'd be lost, too."

Benny sighed with disappointment. "That means we've come to a dead end."

"Maybe not, Benny," Violet said, smiling a little. "Maybe not."

CHAPTER 7

The Ghost Chase

"What are you thinking, Violet?" Jessie asked.

"I have a hunch the next clue is right here in the house."

"But, Violet," Benny protested, "the arrow was pointing to the tree house. Remember?"

"That's true, Benny," Violet said. "But the *name* of the tree house is Little St. Ives. What if *that's* the clue to follow?"

"What do you mean, Violet?" Jessie asked.

"Come and see!" Violet led the way to Fran's workroom. After flipping on the light, she made a beeline for the framed verses on the wall. "This one is called *A Little St. Ives Rhyme*," she said, pointing.

The others went to take a closer look. "What does it say?" Benny wanted to know. The youngest Alden was just learning to read.

Henry read aloud over Violet's shoulder:

"As I was going to St. Ives
I met a man with seven wives,
Every wife had seven sacks,
Every sack had seven cats,
Every cat had seven kits,
Kits, cats, sacks, wives,
How many were going to St. Ives?"

"Hey, it's a riddle!" cried Benny, his voice rising with excitement.

"And that's not all," added Violet. "There's even a border of pressed buttercups around it."

"The mysterious box was covered with buttercups, too," Benny realized.

"I think you might be onto something, Violet." Henry sounded just as excited as his brother.

"Yippee!" Benny let out a cheer. "We found the third riddle!"

"Sure looks that way," agreed Henry.

"Way to go, Violet!" Jessie gave her sister an affectionate nudge.

"But . . . what's the answer to this riddle?" Benny wondered. "There sure are a whole lot going to St. Ives."

Jessie thought for a moment. "Well . . . seven wives . . . plus seven sacks . . . plus seven cats . . . plus — "

"Hold on a minute, Jessie," Henry interrupted. "It says *every* wife had seven sacks. That makes it seven wives and *forty-nine* sacks!"

Jessie nodded. "You're right, Henry."

"So how many does *that* make?" asked Benny.

Henry went over to Fran's desk. He

found a pad of paper and a pencil, then sat down to do some figuring. The others gathered around and waited quietly. Henry's lips moved slightly as he added up the numbers. After a while, he looked up.

"One man, plus seven wives, plus forty-nine sacks, plus three-hundred-and-forty-three cats, plus two-thousand, four-hundred-and-one kits." He looked around at his brother and sisters. "The grand total comes to two thousand, eight hundred and one."

"Oops," said Benny. "I think you left somebody out, Henry."

Henry looked puzzled. "I did?" He checked his numbers again.

"You forgot the man — or woman — who met them!" Benny said.

Henry smiled at his little brother. "Good thinking, Benny," he said. "So that makes it two thousand, eight hundred and *two*."

"*That's* our next clue?" Jessie couldn't believe it.

"I guess we didn't find the third riddle after all." Violet sighed. "That one's just silly.

Looks like we're on the wrong track again."

"Never mind," Henry said as they headed up the stairs to bed. "It was a good try."

Benny, who was a few steps ahead, suddenly stopped and turned. "Hear that?" he whispered. His eyes were huge.

"Hear what, Benny?" asked Henry.

Clang, clang. Clang, clang, clang.

This time they all heard it. The sound seemed to be coming from outside. It would stop, only to start again a moment later.

"It's Buttercup!" whispered Benny, sounding anxious.

Henry wasn't having any of that. "We can't be sure that was even a cowbell, Benny," he said as he hurried back downstairs and into the living room. The others followed close behind. They all huddled around and peered out the window into the moonlit garden.

Clang, clang. Clang, clang, clang.

"Oh, that *is* a cowbell!" cried Violet. "And it's the exact same clanging I heard last night!" She quickly told the others about the old cowbell at Roback's Antique Shop.

"That made the same sound, too," she said firmly.

"Even so, Violet," Henry said after a moment's thought, "that doesn't mean there's a *ghost* cow out there."

"I asked Cora if stray cows ever wander into town," Violet informed them. "She said she's never heard of it."

Clang, clang. Clang, clang, clang.

"Well, *somebody's* ringing that bell," Jessie pointed out.

"There's only one way to find out who." Henry squared his shoulders and headed out of the room. The other Aldens followed at his heels.

The four children opened and closed the front door behind them quietly. Henry and Jessie were in the lead as they started across the grass; Violet and Benny followed close behind. All of a sudden, Henry stopped so quickly that Jessie almost ran right into him.

Clang, clang. Clang, clang, clang.

"Uh-oh," said Benny, backing up. His heart was pounding.

Henry pointed. Was that a shadow moving across the yard? "Who's there?" he called out.

The shadowy figure disappeared into the inky darkness of the bushes. The Aldens ran into the bushes, too, but it was too late. It was almost as if the shadowy figure had vanished into thin air.

"I sure wish we had a flashlight," Henry said, as he looked around.

"It's too late now, Henry," Violet told him breathlessly.

As they started back to the house, Benny moved closer to Jessie. She put a comforting arm around his shoulder. "Whoever was ringing that bell is long gone," she assured him.

"Do you think anybody else heard the bell?" Benny wondered, as they had a late-night meeting in the room that Violet and Jessie were sharing.

"Maybe, Benny," said Jessie, "but I doubt it. Fran said she was a sound sleeper."

Henry nodded. "And Lottie seemed very tired."

"I just can't understand somebody pulling a prank like that." Violet couldn't stop shaking her head. "Who would do such a thing?"

Henry had a thought. "What about Nelson?" When he saw the look of surprise on everyone's face, he added, "Maybe he thinks it's the only way to get Fran to sell her house."

"By convincing her that Shadowbox really *is* haunted?" Jessie shot her older brother a disbelieving glance. "By a *cow*?"

"It's possible," said Henry.

"I can't imagine Nelson doing anything so awful to his mother," argued Violet.

Jessie had an opinion about this. "Maybe he's trying to scare *us* away."

"That's an interesting theory, Jessie," said Henry. "But the only reason he would try to scare us is to keep us from solving the mystery."

"Well, he wasn't very happy about us helping with it," Jessie pointed out. "Maybe he wants to solve the mystery himself."

That made sense to Henry. "Nelson *does*

think money is important. At least, that's what Fran said. Maybe he's hoping to keep the treasure for himself."

"You know," said Violet, "Nelson isn't the only suspect."

The others turned to her, puzzled.

"I think we should include Cora Roback on our list."

Benny looked confused. "But, Violet, Cora thinks the whole idea of a ghost cow is silly."

"Maybe she's trying to prove that to Fran," Violet suggested. She was sitting on the window seat with her arms around her knees.

The others had to admit that was possible. Didn't Cora think all the other sightings had been staged? Maybe she was trying to convince Fran the ghost was a fake by showing her how easy it would be to fool people.

"And she owns an antique store," added Jessie. "So it would be easy for her to get hold of an old cowbell."

"It'd be easy for anyone to get hold of a

cowbell," Henry pointed out. "Cedarburg is overflowing with antique stores."

"I still think Lottie is behind everything," insisted Benny. "I bet she's trying to scare us away so *she* can beat us to the treasure."

"You might be right, Benny," Jessie said. "She does need money for school in the fall."

"And she never lets anyone see what she's painting," added Benny. "What's that all about?"

"Maybe she's shy about her work," offered Violet.

Jessie frowned. She thought there was more to it than that, but she didn't say anything.

"There's one other person we should consider," Henry told them. "Somebody who wants everyone to believe Shadowbox is haunted."

"Who's that, Henry?" Violet asked.

"Fran," Henry said.

"Fran!" The others were so surprised, all they could do was stare at their older brother with their mouths open.

"You don't mean that, do you, Henry?" said Jessie. "You can't really be suspicious of Fran."

Henry looked around at them. "We have to consider everybody."

"But why would she want to fool us, Henry?" Violet's soft eyes were serious. "She's been so nice to us."

"We all like her," said Henry, keeping his voice low. "But still . . . she *is* proud of her family ghost."

Jessie nodded slowly. "And she likes to entertain visitors."

"Maybe we should keep a lid on this for now," Henry suggested. "I think we should try to figure out a few things on our own first." The others agreed.

"What if Buttercup really *is* trying to tell Fran something?" said Benny.

Jessie, who was sitting on the bed right next to him, gave her little brother a hug. "That was no ghost out there, Benny," she assured him. Still, it did make her wonder.

CHAPTER 8

How Many Were Going to St. Ives?

The next morning, the four Aldens joined Fran for breakfast on the back patio. Lottie had left early for work, so the umbrella table was set for five. With the sun shining and the birds chirping, they munched happily on blueberry muffins, cold cereal, and fresh strawberries. The children put all thoughts of the runaway ghost aside for a while — at least until Fran said the strangest thing.

"It seems the old photograph of

Homer has disappeared," she announced.

"What?" Henry held a spoonful of cereal in midair. "Are you sure?"

"Quite sure, Henry," Fran said as she poured herself a cup of coffee. "I searched high and low for it this morning, but I couldn't find it anywhere. Oh, it's gone, all right."

"I can't believe it!" said Violet, her eyes wide. "Who could have taken it?"

Benny swallowed a mouthful of muffin. "I know who."

All eyes turned to the youngest Alden. "Who, Benny?" asked Jessie.

"A thief. That's who!"

Fran held up a hand. "Now, now, Benny, let's not jump to any conclusions."

Nodding, Jessie took a sip of her orange juice. "We can't be certain it was actually *stolen*."

"Besides," Violet added, "why would anyone want to steal an old photograph of Fran's relatives?"

"You're right, Violet," Henry said after a moment's thought. "It doesn't make sense."

As Fran helped herself to another muffin, a frown crossed her kind face. "Visitors are always curious about the man who painted *The Runaway Ghost.* I was planning to get the photograph enlarged. That way, folks could see what Homer looked like."

"Don't worry, Fran," Jessie assured her. "We'll look for it after breakfast."

"Thanks anyway, Jessie, but there's no need to waste your time like that. I've already given the place a thorough going-over."

"Wow, that makes three mysteries!" Benny pointed out.

Fran looked puzzled. "Three mysteries?"

Violet nudged her little brother under the table. Now Benny remembered — he wasn't supposed to mention the cowbell ringing in the night.

Changing the subject, Jessie said, "I sure hope the photograph turns up soon."

"So do I," Fran replied. Then she added, "The gallery phoned, so I'm off to town again. They need a fresh supply of my greeting cards."

"Maybe we could lend a hand," Violet volunteered. She remembered how tired Fran had been after their walking tour of Cedarburg.

"We could deliver the cards for you," Jessie was quick to agree.

"Oh, you wouldn't mind?" Fran looked relieved.

"We'll get your cards there in a flash!" promised Benny.

This made Henry smile a little. "Well, we'll get them there safe and sound, that's for sure."

After breakfast, Fran scribbled the address on a piece of paper. "The Creekside Gallery is right in the middle of town. You can't miss it."

Henry folded the paper that Fran handed him. Then he carefully put the address in his pocket.

"I'm sure Amanda will be pleased." Fran handed the Aldens two old shoeboxes from the counter. CARDS BY FRAN was written across each in blue ink. "There are plenty here. Enough to keep the gallery stocked for a while, I think."

"We can use my backpack to carry them," Jessie offered.

As they set off for town, Violet said, "Poor Fran! That was her only photograph of Homer."

Benny frowned. "I wonder why Lottie stole it."

"Benny!" Jessie exclaimed. "We shouldn't suspect people until we're certain it was actually stolen."

After a moment's thought, Violet said, "It does seem odd, though, that it suddenly disappeared."

"I think we should concentrate on one mystery at a time," suggested Henry.

"You're right, Henry," Jessie agreed. "And finding that treasure for Fran comes first."

When they reached the Creekside Gallery, the Aldens looked at each other in surprise. It was the same gallery where Lottie worked. "It looks like Lottie's got another customer," said Benny, peering through the window. "Only this time it's a lady in a big straw hat."

As they stepped inside, Jessie reminded her little brother, "Let's keep out of her way while she's working."

A smartly dressed woman was standing behind the counter. She looked up when the Aldens approached. "May I help you?" she asked.

The youngest Alden sprang forward. "We're the Speedy Alden Delivery Service," he announced. "And we brought something from Fran."

The salesclerk gave Benny an amused smile. "My name's Amanda, and I'm sure glad you came so fast. As of this morning, Fran's cards are completely sold out."

After introductions had been made, Jessie tugged the shoeboxes from her backpack. "There should be enough here to last a while," she said cheerfully, as she placed the boxes on the counter. "At least, that's what Fran says."

Amanda was looking inside one of the boxes. "She really has the magic touch, doesn't she?" She held up a greeting card. Pressed forget-me-nots and lavender had been arranged to form a delicate heart-shaped design on the front.

Violet gasped. "Oh, it's beautiful!"

Amanda flashed them a smile. "I guarantee this batch won't be on the shelf for long."

Benny, who was glancing around, suddenly touched Henry's arm. "Hey, that man was here yesterday!"

"What man?" Henry asked.

"Over there." Benny nodded toward a customer at the far end of the gallery. "Wasn't he sitting across from Lottie yesterday?"

Henry shrugged a little. "It's hard to tell."

The man, who was studying a painting on the back wall, was broad-shouldered and had dark hair. Although his back was to them, he looked vaguely familiar. Suddenly the man turned around.

"Look, he has a beard," Benny whispered loudly. "That *is* the same man."

Hearing this, Amanda said, "That's Rally

Jensen. He's an art collector from out of town. Actually, he's been in here quite a bit lately." She lowered her voice and leaned closer. "I'm hoping he'll purchase a painting before he leaves tomorrow," she added, crossing her fingers.

"I'm sure he will," Violet said. She glanced around admiringly at the colorful canvases hanging on the walls. "You have some beautiful artwork."

Amanda beamed. "We only display the very best."

"Violet's an artist, too," said Benny proudly.

Amanda's eyebrows rose. "Oh?"

Violet smiled shyly. "I *do* like to sketch and draw."

"Well, I'm glad you told me." Amanda bent down to rummage around beneath the counter. "I have some reading material you might find interesting, Violet." Straightening up, she held out a handful of brochures. "You'll find a ton of information about artists in these," she said. "Please help yourself. They're just cluttering things up around here."

"Thank you!" Violet's face lit up.

Everyone glanced through the brochures except Benny. He was too busy looking around at the other people in the gallery. The lady in the big straw hat was going out the door with the sketch Lottie drew of her. When she left, the art collector went over to Lottie and began to talk quietly.

Benny watched as Fran's boarder listened to what the man was saying. She was pale and she looked upset. The man suddenly turned on his heel and started for the door. "Remember, it's tonight or never!" he called back over his shoulder. Then he left.

"Did you hear that?" Benny whispered to Henry.

"Yes," his brother answered. Jessie and Violet had heard it, too.

Lottie slumped down in her chair, her chin in her hands. She did not look happy. She sat very still for a moment. Then, as if feeling the children's eyes on her, she looked up. The Aldens could tell by the look on her face that Lottie was startled to see them. In a flash, she was on her feet and out the door, leaving the children to stare after her.

The Aldens thanked Amanda and left the gallery.

Outside, they turned to one another. "That was very strange," Benny said. "Lottie didn't even say hi to us."

"She's acting very suspiciously," Jessie added.

Henry agreed. "You'd think we'd just caught her in the middle of something she wanted to keep secret."

"That man, Rally Jensen, said it was tonight or never," Benny reminded them as they started back to Shadowbox. "I wonder what he meant by that."

Henry shrugged. "There's no way of knowing."

"Do you think Lottie's up to something?" Benny wondered.

"Yes," Jessie answered with a quick nod. "We just don't know what."

"You can't be sure of that, Jessie." Violet didn't like to think the young artist would do anything wrong. "Rally Jensen's an art collector. For all we know, Lottie might be planning to show him some of her art before he leaves town."

Jessie turned to her sister. "But, Violet, that doesn't explain her reaction. Whatever that man was whispering, it seemed to really upset her."

"It *is* suspicious," Violet admitted. "But I don't think we should jump to any conclusions."

"I suppose you're right," Jessie said, backing down a little. Violet had a point. It was one thing to suspect somebody, it was another thing to have proof. Still, she couldn't shake the feeling that something wasn't right.

"I'm not sure I trust Lottie," Henry said. "I think we should keep an eye on her for a while." The others agreed.

Benny's face suddenly broke into a grin as four small black dogs came toward them. A teenage boy in a green-and-yellow base-

ball cap was holding onto their leashes.

"You sure are lucky to have four dogs!" Benny told the teenager.

"They're not mine," the boy answered. "I just walk them for a neighbor."

"Oh, too bad," Benny said, as one of the puppies licked his hand.

The teenager shrugged. "I'm a dog-walker. That's what I do for the summer."

"Cool job," said Henry.

"Yeah, I guess it's all right." He turned to Benny. "You can pet them if you want."

"Thanks!" Benny was all smiles as he dropped to the ground. The dogs began to wag their tails as he scratched them behind the ears.

"We have a little dog at home," Violet told the boy shyly. "His name's Watch."

The teenager wiped the sweat from his forehead. "Well, I'd better go. I have to take the dogs to the park." Then he hurried away.

"I'm going to be a dogwalker when I grow up," Benny announced, as he ran along beside Henry. "And a detective."

"You're already a dogwalker, Benny," Violet pointed out. "We're always taking Watch for walks."

"And you're a pretty good detective already," Jessie reminded her little brother.

Violet frowned in thought. "I just wonder if we'll solve the case we're on now."

"It's going to be much harder than we thought," admitted Jessie.

Henry nodded as he turned to face Jessie. "A tree house called Little St. Ives isn't much to go on."

They were deep in thought when Benny began to chant, "When we were going to Shadowbox, we met a boy and four dogs out for a walk. How many were going to Shadowbox?"

They all laughed at their little brother's funny riddle.

Benny added everything up on his fingers. "The four of us . . . plus the boy . . . plus four puppies. That makes nine going to Shadowbox!"

"Not quite, Benny." Henry smiled and

shook his head. "Only the four of us are going to Shadowbox. The boy and the dogs are going the other way."

"Oh, I didn't think of that," said Benny.

Jessie suddenly snapped her fingers. "That's it!"

Henry turned and gave Jessie a confused look. "What's it?"

"I know how many were going to St. Ives!"

"We already figured that out," Benny reminded her.

"Well, I'm pretty sure we got it wrong," Jessie said excitedly. "Remember how the riddle goes?" She began to recite, *"When I was going to St. Ives/ I met a man with seven wives."* She paused for a moment to let them think about it. "Don't you see?" she said at last. "What if the man and his wives — and their sacks and cats and kits — were all going in the opposite direction?"

"Then only the person who met them is going to St. Ives!" cried Benny.

"Exactly!" said Jessie. "And that means, the answer to the riddle is *one*."

Henry nodded. "You must be right, Jessie."

"So the number one is our next clue?" Violet looked puzzled. "What kind of clue is that?"

"And where's it leading us?" added Henry.

"I think I know," Benny said, breaking into a run. "Come on!" He motioned for the others to follow.

CHAPTER 9

Saved by the Bell

"The answer to the riddle is one," Benny called back as he rounded the corner, racing for Shadowbox. "And Buttercup has the number one on her bell!"

"You think the answer to the riddle has something to do with Buttercup?" Violet asked, running right behind him.

"I'm sure of it," Benny said. "We just have to . . . oh, no!" Benny stopped suddenly at the top of the driveway.

"What?" Jessie asked, trying to catch her breath.

"The riddle leads us straight to Buttercup," Benny explained, "but Buttercup isn't around anymore. And that means — "

"We've come to another dead end," finished Violet.

Just then, they heard a familiar voice drifting out the open window of Shadowbox. It was Grandfather!

Benny rushed inside, arms outstretched. Grandfather was standing in the hallway with Fran. He laughed and returned the hug.

"Grandfather, you're back!" Jessie hugged him, too.

"I finished my work sooner than expected," Grandfather told them, embracing Violet and Henry. Then everyone was talking at once.

"I bought a ghost cookie cutter," Benny told him.

"We played croquet on the back lawn last night," Jessie said.

"Fran showed us how to press flowers," Violet was saying.

"We've been trying to solve a mystery," added Henry.

Grandfather chuckled. "Sounds like you've been busy."

As they sat down to lunch, Fran turned to Grandfather. "Let's do something special tonight. How does a picnic supper in the park sound? A local group's performing in the band shell."

Grandfather thought an outdoor concert sounded great. So did everyone else.

"You know, it's been ages since I've seen Nelson," Grandfather said. "Why not invite him along tonight?"

It took Fran a moment to answer, but when she did, she was smiling. "That's exactly what I'll do, James. Thanks to Violet," she added, "I've come to realize how little time Nelson and I spend together these days."

"Maybe we could invite Reese and her mother, too," suggested Jessie.

"Yes, I might as well mend all my bridges." Fran nodded. "Oh, and I must remember to phone Lottie. She can meet us at the park after work."

Benny swallowed a bite of his ham sandwich. "And we can bring the croquet set along, too." He sounded excited.

After lunch, Grandfather went upstairs to take a nap. The children cleared the table while Fran made her phone calls. Cora accepted Fran's invitation eagerly. So did Nelson. Lottie was the only one who had other plans. The Aldens couldn't help wondering if her plans had anything to do with Rally Jensen, the art collector.

When the kitchen was spic and span, the children joined Fran in her workroom. Fran passed out heavy stationery, folded in half. "The flowers are very delicate, so handle them carefully," she advised.

Violet decided on a border of purple pansies on the front of her card. Henry made a zigzag design with goldenrod and the dark green tendrils of a morning glory. Jessie draped red velvet ribbon through a wreath of creamy elder blossoms. And Benny used bright yellow buttercups to form the letter *B*.

They were just finishing when Grandfather poked his head into the room. "So this is where everyone's hiding."

The children smiled proudly as Grandfather oohed and aahed over their greeting cards.

"I bet you didn't know your grandchildren were so talented, did you, James?" Fran said, her eyes shining.

At that, Grandfather had to laugh. "Fran, my grandchildren never cease to amaze me!"

"I guess we'll never find the treasure." Benny sighed as he added a spoonful of mayonnaise to the potato salad. "Not without Buttercup to lead us to it."

The four Alden children were busy in the kitchen. They had offered to prepare the picnic supper while Grandfather and Fran sat outside and chatted about old times.

"I wish the runaway ghost would give us a clue," Benny added.

Henry looked up. "Wait a minute!" he said. "You might be onto something, Benny."

"Ghosts don't exist, Henry," Violet said. "Remember?"

"Yes, but Fran's *painting* of the runaway ghost is real," explained Henry.

"Of course!" Jessie said. She jumped out of her seat and gave Henry a high five. "Maybe that's where the third riddle is leading us!" The four Aldens made a beeline for Fran's living room.

No one spoke for a moment as they stared up at the bell around Buttercup's neck. Then Violet said, "Fran's hunch was right. The mystery really *is* connected to Buttercup."

"I don't understand," Benny said. "Where's the treasure?"

Violet looked thoughtful. "Maybe the painting is the treasure," she said.

Henry shook his head. "I doubt it. Fran says the painting's not worth very much."

"There must be something we're not seeing," insisted Violet.

"Maybe Lottie was right," Jessie suggested.

"About what?" Benny asked.

"About the mystery just being a parlor game," said Jessie. "Maybe Anne just made it up to entertain her children, and there isn't a real treasure at the end."

"And maybe the clues just lead to the painting of their treasured pet," Henry said slowly, figuring it out as he talked.

"Then Buttercup's the treasure?" Benny looked confused.

Henry shrugged a little. "It's beginning to look that way."

But Violet wasn't so sure. She had a nagging feeling there was more to it than that. Could the answer lie somewhere in the painting itself?

"Wow, there sure are a lot of people here," Benny said as he looked around the park.

Everyone was enjoying the beautiful evening. But no one was enjoying it more than the Aldens and their friends. With the band playing nearby, they ate their supper and talked and joked. Even Nelson, wearing shorts and a T-shirt, was all smiles. People said hello as they passed, and many of them knew Fran and Nelson by name.

After they had finished eating, Grandfather headed over to the covered stage to listen to the music with Cora and Reese. Fran went for a stroll along the creek with her son. Henry, Jessie, and Benny started a game of croquet.

Violet decided to sit it out. She wanted to look at the gallery brochures she'd brought with her. She thumbed through them quickly, then settled on one about great American artists. The painting on the cover of the brochure caught her attention. "Hey, look!" she called to the others. "Here's a painting of a croquet game!"

Benny, Jessie, and Henry crowded around to study the picture. Three young ladies in hats and long dresses were playing croquet. A young man in a brown jacket and beige trousers was on one knee, placing a croquet ball on the grass. He was wearing a straw hat, and he had a mustache.

Benny giggled. "They're dressed just like the people in Fran's photo of Homer."

"I guess that was the style back then," Henry said.

Violet leaned in for a closer look at the people's faces. Then she gasped. "That's them!" she said.

"Who?" asked Jessie.

"That's Selden and Anne!" Violet said, excitedly. "They look just like that in the missing photograph."

Jessie took another look at the painting. "Now that you mention it," she said, "that man does look a lot like Selden."

"And see the lady in the background?" put in Violet. "The one in the brown dress? She sure looks like Anne, don't you think?"

"Why isn't Homer in the painting?" Benny wanted to know. "He was in the photograph."

Henry, who was sprawled out on the blanket, propped himself up on one elbow.

"This is getting stranger and stranger. What does it say in the brochure, Violet?"

Violet couldn't help laughing at herself. "I never thought to read the article." As she quickly scanned the brochure, she came across something that made her eyes widen.

"What is it?" Henry asked.

"Well, maybe this is just a weird coincidence," Violet began, "but the artist who painted this was named Winslow *Homer*!"

Everyone was so surprised that no one said anything for a minute. Then Benny asked, "Are you sure Homer wasn't his *first* name?"

"Quite sure, Benny," said Violet. "It says that Winslow Homer painted the *Croquet Scene* in 1866."

"That's the same year *The Runaway Ghost* was painted," Henry pointed out.

"Fran said she doesn't know much about Selden's friend," Jessie said after a moment's thought. "Maybe she just assumed Homer was his first name, since that's what Selden called him."

"That makes sense," agreed Henry.

"Homer was a common first name in the olden days."

"I can't believe it." Violet's eyes were huge. "Selden's friend was the great American artist, Winslow Homer!"

Jessie put one hand up to her mouth. "Homer's not in that *Croquet Scene* because . . . he was painting it!"

"Then . . . that means — " began Benny.

Henry cut in. "It means Fran's painting is worth a fortune!"

"I just wish we could compare this picture with the missing photograph," Violet said. "Then we would know for sure if it's really Selden and Anne in the *Croquet Scene*."

"Let's look for it when we get back," Henry said. "Maybe we have sharper eyes than Fran."

"We'll never find it," said Benny. "Somebody stole it."

"Well, we ought to try to prove it before we tell Fran," Jessie said. "Remember what Nelson said about getting her hopes up."

The others agreed.

When the concert ended, Fran invited

everyone back to Shadowbox for dessert. It was already dark when they joined the streams of people leaving the park.

Back at Shadowbox, everyone followed Fran to the living room. She flipped on a light switch and light filled the cheery room. Fran stepped through the doorway, then she stopped abruptly when she noticed someone sitting in one of the buttercup-patterned chairs.

It was Lottie. She was holding a large, flat package wrapped in brown paper on her lap, and there was a suitcase beside her chair. Violet wondered how long the young artist had been sitting all alone in the dark.

"Lottie?" said Fran. "Is everything all right?"

"I'm afraid I have to leave," Lottie answered nervously. "There's been a . . . a family emergency."

"Oh, dear!" cried Fran.

"Is there anything we can do?" asked Violet.

"Do you need a ride to the airport?" offered Nelson.

Lottie shook her head as she got up. "A friend of mine agreed to give me a lift."

Everyone offered their sympathy — everyone except Benny. He wasn't paying attention. He was staring at the painting above the fireplace. It was exactly as it had always been, Shadowbox peeking out from among the trees and Buttercup grazing nearby. And yet, the youngest Alden was sure there was something wrong. When he took a step closer to the painting, he noticed what it was.

The number one was missing from Buttercup's bell!

CHAPTER 10

A Message from the Past

"It . . . it's gone!" exclaimed Benny.

Everyone turned to him. "What's gone?" Jessie asked.

"The number one on Buttercup's bell!" Benny was staring at the painting with wide, unbelieving eyes.

"Oh!" Violet came up behind her little brother. "Benny's right. The number one has disappeared!"

The Alden children looked at each other, their eyes round. What on earth was going on? Did this have something to do with the mystery riddles?

"But how could . . . " Fran's eyebrows furrowed as she stared at the painting.

Before the children could answer, Grandfather said, "Maybe it's not the same painting."

Fran sank down into a chair. "I . . . I don't understand."

As Reese placed a gentle hand on Fran's shoulder, Cora turned to Grandfather and said, "Are you implying someone stole the original painting and . . . and replaced it with a fake?" She looked doubtful.

Henry and Jessie exchanged glances. Had someone else figured out that the painting was a treasure?

"Why in the world would anyone steal it?" argued Nelson. "That old painting wasn't worth a thing."

"It was to me," corrected Fran, burying her head in her hands.

"And to anyone hoping to make some quick cash," put in Henry.

Nelson looked over at him. "Quick cash?"

"Selling it to an art collector, I mean," Henry explained.

"Someone like Rally Jensen," Jessie added, watching Lottie closely. "I bet he'd pay a lot of money for that painting."

Fran slowly lifted her head. "What? Why?"

"We solved the mystery, Fran," Jessie explained. "The clues led us straight to *The Runaway Ghost* painting."

Violet nodded. "It turned out to be the treasure."

"Only, now it's gone." Benny scratched his head. "The number one was on Buttercup's bell just before we went to the park. I saw it with my own eyes!"

"That means the painting was taken while we were out," Grandfather reasoned. "The thief couldn't have gone far."

"You're right, Grandfather," said Henry. "The thief is still close by." He gave Lottie a meaningful look. "And so is the painting."

Lottie's eyes darted from side to side. Then she suddenly rushed toward the door. But Grandfather was too quick for her. "Don't even think about leaving, young lady," he told her, blocking the way.

Fran was so startled she needed a few moments to collect her thoughts. "What's this all about?"

As Lottie turned and faced everyone, she forced a tense laugh. "I have no idea what you're talking about."

Benny eyed her package suspiciously. "What have you got wrapped up there?"

"Now look here," Lottie began sternly. "This is *my* painting. It's the one — " She stopped talking. Her shoulders slumped and she sat down in a chair, looking defeated. Tearing the wrapping away from the canvas, she revealed the painting of *The Runaway Ghost*.

"I think you have some explaining to do," said Grandfather.

After a moment's silence, Lottie began to speak. "I'm sorry, Fran. I did it for the

money. I told myself you'd never notice," she confessed.

"But *we* noticed," Benny said.

Jessie looked at Lottie. "You figured out that Selden's friend was really Winslow Homer, didn't you?"

Lottie didn't deny it. "I studied all about the great American artists. There was no mistaking Winslow Homer's style — or his signature in the corner of the painting."

Fran looked at her, stunned.

"It's true, Fran," Violet said quietly. "Winslow Homer was your great-great-grandfather's mysterious friend."

Fran's mouth dropped open. She was too shocked to speak.

Jessie turned to Lottie. "That explains why you wouldn't show anyone what you were painting in your room. You were making a copy of *The Runaway Ghost*, weren't you?"

"Yes, I admit it," said Lottie. "I took some snapshots of the painting and copied it in secret. I was desperate to make enough money for school. The only problem was time." She avoided looking Fran in the eye. "I needed time to get the details right."

"But Rally Jensen is leaving town tomorrow," said Henry, urging her on. "So you had to finish quickly."

"Yes," Lottie said, looking surprised that Henry knew that. "Rally was willing to pay a great deal of money for the original painting. It seemed simple enough. Nobody at Shadowbox had a clue this was an original Winslow Homer. So . . . I figured, what was the harm in making a switch?"

Violet smiled sadly. No wonder Lottie had been so upset the other night. She must have thought they were on to her when Jessie asked if it was hard making that kind of switch.

Benny frowned. "Your plan almost worked, too."

Lottie looked at Benny and nodded. "I hadn't counted on the Aldens being such good detectives."

"What about the photograph of Homer?" Violet asked. "Did you take it?"

"Yes." Lottie reached into her purse and

took out the old photograph. "This looks a lot like one of Homer's other paintings. I was afraid somebody might see this and figure it out."

Cora nodded. "And that's why you were so quick to agree with me about that magazine article," she guessed. "You didn't want *The Runaway Ghost* painting to get any publicity."

Henry had something to add. "You even tried to convince us the mystery riddle was just a silly parlor game," he said.

Lottie nodded. "I knew there was a treasure hanging right there, above the fireplace. I didn't want anyone to find out."

Fran hadn't said a word while Lottie had been telling her story. Now she spoke up, her face pained. "I know it isn't easy putting yourself through school, Lottie. But that doesn't make it okay to steal." She looked as if she really couldn't believe what Lottie had done.

Lottie twisted her hands in her lap. "I really didn't want to steal from you, Fran. You've always been so kind to me." Her voice wavered. "I know you won't believe this, but I was about to put the painting back when you came through the door."

"Then why did you try to make a run for it?" Nelson sounded doubtful.

"I panicked." Lottie threw her hands up.

"Lottie *was* still sitting here in the dark," Violet was quick to point out.

Fran thought about this for a moment. "Yes, I suppose you could have been long gone, Lottie," she said at last. "You deserve the benefit of the doubt, so I'm not going to call the police. I don't believe you had your heart in being a thief."

Lottie's face crumbled. "I'm so sorry I betrayed your trust, Fran."

"If you mean that," replied Fran, "then you'll learn from your mistakes, and you'll never do anything like this again."

Looking truly regretful, Lottie walked slowly from the room and out of the house.

"I guess it *was* Lottie ringing that cowbell in the night," concluded Benny. "But why?"

Fran raised an eyebrow. "Cowbell?"

Reese's face turned red. "No, that was my idea."

"It was your idea to scare us?" Benny looked upset.

Reese looked over at the Aldens sheepishly. "I wanted everyone to think the runaway ghost had come back. I got one of the old cowbells from my mother's antique store, and I rang it in the middle of the night."

"But why?" Cora asked, looking confused. "Why would you do such a thing, Reese?"

Violet thought she knew the answer. "You wanted your mother to include Buttercup in her article, right?"

Nodding, Reese hung her head and stared at the floor. "I thought they would if . . . if everyone was suddenly talking about the runaway ghost."

Cora put an arm around her daughter. "I know you were just trying to help Fran, Reese," she said. "But that wasn't the way to do it."

"I'm sorry if I frightened you, Benny," Reese apologized.

"Oh, I knew it wasn't a *real* ghost," said Benny. "Right, Henry?"

"Right, Benny," Henry answered, hiding a smile.

It wasn't long before everyone was sipping lemonade and munching on chocolate cake. Nelson smiled as he looked over at Winslow Homer's painting, hanging above the fireplace once again.

"It really *is* a remarkable work of art," he commented.

Fran seemed surprised to hear this. "But . . . you always wanted me to put something a little more modern up there, Nelson. Something with more pizzazz, remember?"

"Yes, it seems to me I did say that," Nelson recalled, laughing a little. "On more than one occasion."

"Just imagine," said Cora. "We're looking at an original Winslow Homer!"

Nelson took a sip of lemonade. "The past

really does hold some wonderful treasures," he said. The ice clinked in his glass.

Fran nodded, her face beaming.

Henry was wondering about something. "What will you do with the painting, Fran?"

"You'll have lots of pennies to rub together if you sell it," put in Benny.

After a few moments, Fran went over to the fireplace. "This painting should be enjoyed by everyone," she said, as she buffed the brass plaque attached to the frame. "I'll make sure *The Runaway Ghost* finds a home in one of the finest museums in Wisconsin."

Nelson opened his mouth as if about to argue. But then he closed it again. He said only, "Whatever makes you happy, Mother."

Just then, Fran suddenly exclaimed, "What on earth . . . ?"

The others turned to look at her. "What is it?" asked Cora.

"This plaque's a bit loose," Fran said. "And . . . there seems to be something tucked into a small opening just beneath it."

While everyone watched in amazement, she pulled out a folded piece of paper, yellowed with age.

"What is it?" Benny asked, bouncing with excitement.

Fran carefully unfolded the paper, then read the words aloud:

"Dearest children,

If you are reading this letter, then you have solved the riddles and found this painting hidden in the Buttercup Room. Although our good friend, Winslow Homer, never laid eyes on our treasured pet, he has managed to capture Buttercup's likeness exactly — right down to the number one on her bell! It's enough to make you believe in ghosts, isn't it?

Your loving mother, Anne."

"So the mystery really *was* just a parlor game," Jessie realized. "Anne just wanted her children to have some fun finding the painting."

"There's something I don't understand."

Benny looked puzzled. "If the mysterious box was still under the floorboards, how was the mystery solved?"

That was a good question. It was clear Anne's children had never found the box of clues. So how had Winslow Homer's painting come to hang on the wall in the living room?

"Anne died from pneumonia the winter of 1866," Fran said after a moment's thought. "It's possible she became ill before giving her children the first riddle."

"Oh, no!" cried Violet.

Fran went on, "Somebody probably came across the painting of *The Runaway Ghost* when the old mudroom was torn down years later."

"I guess the answer to the last riddle was supposed to lead to the Buttercup Room," Henry concluded.

Grandfather nodded. "Anne probably had no idea the painting itself would be worth a fortune one day."

"And when it was finally found," added

Cora, "I imagine nobody knew the real artist was the great Winslow Homer."

"Well, thanks to the Aldens, the mystery has finally been solved," said Fran. "And I have a lot more to add to that article I'm writing."

Cora blinked in surprise. "You're writing an article?"

Fran nodded. "For the historical magazine. It's all about the runaway ghost."

The Alden children looked at one another. That was what Fran had meant when she said she wasn't going to sit around and do nothing. If Cora wouldn't write about Buttercup, then *she* would!

Benny looked over at the painting. "Did Winslow Homer really paint a *ghost*?" he asked.

"I don't know, Benny," Fran said with a wink. "It's a mystery."

GERTRUDE CHANDLER WARNER discovered when she was teaching that many readers who like an exciting story could find no books that were both easy and fun to read. She decided to try to meet this need, and her first book, *The Boxcar Children*, quickly proved she had succeeded.

Miss Warner drew on her own experiences to write the mystery. As a child she spent hours watching trains go by on the tracks opposite her family home. She often dreamed about what it would be like to set up housekeeping in a caboose or freight car — the situation the Alden children find themselves in.

When Miss Warner received requests for more adventures involving Henry, Jessie, Violet, and Benny Alden, she began additional stories. In each, she chose a special setting and introduced unusual or eccentric characters who liked the unpredictable.

While the mystery element is central to each of Miss Warner's books, she never thought of them as strictly juvenile mysteries. She liked to stress the Aldens' independence and resourcefulness and their solid New England devotion to using up and making do. The Aldens go about most of their adventures with as little adult supervision as possible — something else that delights young readers.

Miss Warner lived in Putnam, Connecticut, until her death in 1979. During her lifetime, she received hundreds of letters from girls and boys telling her how much they liked her books.